Ra

Story Keeper Series
Book 15

Dave and Pat Sargent (*left*) are longtime residents of Prairie Grove, Arkansas. Dave, a fourth-generation dairy farmer, began writing in early December 1990. Pat, a former teacher, began writing in the fourth grade. They enjoy the outdoors and have a real love for animals.

Sue Rogers (*right*) returned to her beloved Mississippi after retirement. She shared books with children for more than thirty years. These stories fulfill a dream of writing books—to continue the sharing.

Rays of the Sun

Story Keeper Series
Book 15

By Dave and Pat Sargent
and Sue Rogers

Beyond "The End"
By Sue Rogers

Illustrated by Jane Lenoir

Ozark Publishing, Inc.
P.O. Box 228
Prairie Grove, AR 72753

Cataloging-in-Publication Data

Sargent, Dave, 1941–
    Rays of the sun / by Dave and Pat Sargent
and Sue Rogers ; illustrated by Jane Lenoir. —
Prairie Grove, AR : Ozark Publishing, c2005.
        p. cm. (Story keeper series ; 15)

    "Learn lessons"—Cover.
    SUMMARY: Wenona, the firstborn daughter
of a Shoshone mother, takes her duties of looking
after her young brother and baby sisters seriously,
though she is only three years old! She becomes a
good cook and earns a special surprise and honor.
    ISBN 1-56763-931-3 (hc)
           1-56763-932-1 (pbk)
    1. Indians of North America—Juvenile
fiction. 2. Shoshone Indians—Juvenile fiction.
[1. Native Americans—United States—Fiction.
2. Shoshone Indians—Fiction.] 1. Sargent,
Pat, 1936– I. Rogers, Sue, 1933– III. Lenoir,
Jane, 1950– ill. IV. Title. V. Series.

    PZ7.S243Ra 2005
    [Fic]—dc21   2003090098

Printed in the United States of America

Inspired by

the way long-ago Shoshone women cooked nutritious meals for their families, though they had never heard of vitamins.

Dedicated to

Sue's mother who taught her to cook; Helen who shares the pleasure; and her daddy who was her first sampler!

Foreword

A Shoshone first daughter has many duties. Wenona is taking care of a brother and two sisters before she is five. She dresses, feeds, and plays with them. Her good cooking earns her and her family a special surprise and honor.

Contents

If you would like to have the authors of the Story Keeper Series visit your school, free of charge, just call us at 1-800-321-5671 or 1-800-960-3876.

One

Life Journey Begins

On a very warm day while the summer season was walking through our country, my mother and grandmother were gathering rye grass. It came time for my journey of life to begin. In that grass field, my tiny feet were set in the path of my forefathers, the Shoshone.

I was my mother's firstborn daughter. She named me Wenona, which means first daughter.

There was much happiness that night in our house made of poles and woven grass. My mother placed me in the boat basket she had made from river willow. Everyone peeked into my koh'noh (cradleboard). It didn't bother me. I slept through it all.

The next morning my mother faced the sun in the east and sang a prayer song of thanks to Duma Appah for her new daughter.

"Good morning, Grandfather Spirit. All is well. I send you thanks for a beautiful daughter. Walk with her through her journey of life." Mother's words were caught by rays of the sun and carried up to Appah.

The boat basket cradleboard was my home until my neck muscles were strong enough to hold up my head. Then I was kept in the hoop basket until I learned to walk. It kept my backbone and legs straight.

Strapped on Mother's back, I saw the red strawberries she picked. I watched water lilies floating in the pool. I smiled back at yellow sunflowers. Mother talked to me, sang to me, and let me taste things. I saw, touched, heard, tasted, and smelled the things of my people. I was where she was.

Sometimes my basket was propped against a rock, or hung from a tree limb while Mother picked and winnowed pine nuts I watched her hands move to grind the pine nuts into flour.

My mother told me how the pine trees were scattered across our land. "Long ago," she began, "Coyote was out looking for food. His stomach was always empty. He was caught in a blizzard and was freezing to death."

"An old man found him. He cooked a thick warm soup that saved Coyote."

"The sly and curious coyote wanted to find out where the old man got his food. One day he followed the old man. He saw trees with many pine cones. He saw the old man get the pine nuts out of the cones. He saw how he prepared them to make the thick warm soup," she continued.

"Coyote thought, 'Aha! I need some of those trees growing near my home.' He went to the cave where the old man had stored his pine cones. He filled a sack. He wanted to make sure he had enough, so he filled it to the top. It was so heavy he had to drag it over the ground. He didn't care. Away he went with the sack bumping behind him."

"The old man knew Coyote's sneaky ways. He had cut a small hole in the sack. The pine cones fell out of the sack all along the way to Coyote's house. When he got home he had only one pine cone left!"

"That is why Coyote is traveling to this day, looking for food. And that is how the pine nut trees got planted all over our mountains."

Mother gave my basket a rock or two and left me sleeping near where she worked.

Two

A First Daughter's Duties

Rays of the sun took thanks up to Appah for another baby the next year, a boy. Mother named him Istu. Istu means sugar. Grandmother and I call him Sugarlump.

Sugarlump was placed in the boat and hoop baskets where I had spent my first year. He was always near Mother now. Mother taught me how to watch him. I had to turn the basket when the sun was in his eyes. I brushed his hair and washed his face. I learned more and more about taking care of babies.

11

By the time Sugarlump was out of the baskets and crawling, Mother left him in my care. She had to be out gathering food for our family. Taking care of younger brothers and sisters was the older sister's job. By the time five seasons had walked through our country, I was in charge of three little brothers and sisters. I dressed them, fed them and played with them.

I entertained the little ones with games, songs, and stories. The girls liked to watch me juggle a set of three red clay balls, called na-wa-ta-pi ta-na-wa-ta-pi, that Father made for me. I was trying to learn to walk around the children while juggling the balls. Then I could enter juggling contests.

The thing that kept Sugarlump's

attention best was a guessing game. I put a small green stone in one of my hands. I moved it secretly from hand to hand, then held out closed hands for Sugarlump to guess which hand was holding the green stone. He loved it when I opened the hand he tapped and there lay the green stone!

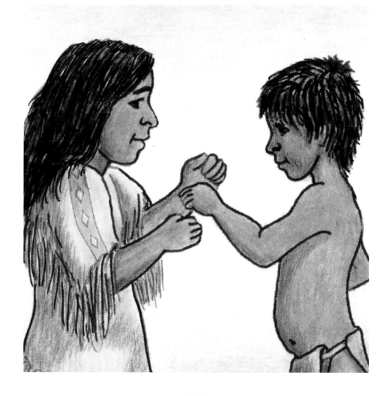

Grandmother taught us to gather and carry wood, water, berries, and seeds. We ran errands and helped care for the elderly. We learned to assume that guests were cold, tired, or hungry. They were to be fed. When they left, they were to be given a gift, with nothing expected in return.

Grandmother and Grandfather were our teachers and storytellers. They taught us to honor and respect our parents and our grandparents. We learned the history, legends, and customs of the Shoshone this way. We learned that the mountains, streams, and plains stand forever.

As a Shoshone first daughter, I had many duties. These duties were given to me at an early age. I was proud to be a Shoshone and to be a first daughter. I was proud that I had seen eight seasons walk around.

One of my duties quickly became the thing that gave me the most pleasure—cooking. From the first time I first helped my mother gather eggs in the marshes and cooked them with ground potatoes, I loved cooking! There was something special about gathering seeds, plants, berries, and roots provided by Mother Earth. Cooking them properly was an art. Inhaling the good smells filled me with satisfaction. The best part was watching my family and guests enjoy a good meal.

The more things I learned to cook, the more supportive Sugarlump became. He was learning all he could about hunting and fishing from Father. He brought squirrels, fish,

rabbits, ducks, geese, and other small
animals and birds to be cooked.

My sisters began to help gather food. They gathered sunflower seeds and wild rice. My youngest sister was good at climbing. She found honey in the fall.

I learned to mix honey with flour ground from pine nuts to make small flat cakes. Every time I met a new woman, I asked how she cooked her favorite food. That is how I learned to add peeled and chopped thistle stalks to soups. They are both crunchy and tasty. My grandfather liked to drink the peppermint tea I brewed. He said it settled his stomach. Grandmother showed me a part of rabbitbrush and milkweed that could be chewed as gum. I found everything about foods and cooking interesting.

Three

The Chief is Coming

Father came bursting into the house one day. His face was flushed. His eyes were dancing. He sent Sugarlump to find Mother. He had news. He asked me to stand beside him.

My thoughts were racing! Had I done something bad? Had I burned his food? Were the mustard seeds bitter? I was almost sick with worry.

Father began. ""First," he said, "My son has seen seven seasons. From this day forward he will be called by his name, Istu."

We all looked at one another while he continued. "A man's son cannot be called a baby name when the Chief is visiting!"

Then he turned to me and said, "The Chief's son ate something you cooked for the festival last spring. He said you would remember."

I blushed. "Yes, Father. He ate the whole basket of cattail cakes," I said. "He didn't say he liked them. He just ate one cake after another."

"The Chief said his son liked them very much, Wenona. He has been searching for someone who can cook them like yours," said Father. "He has found no one. The Chief, his wife, and son are coming for a meal you prepare. This is a great honor, my first daughter. You will have a basket of cattail cakes, won't you?"

"Of course, Father," I answered. "May I be excused now? I want to plan what to cook for the Chief, his wife, and hungry son."

Father took Mother's hand and pulled her up beside him. They were very proud. "This is his oldest son," Father said.

My mother understood. "But our Wenona is so young," I heard her say softly.

The whole village was filled with excitement and activity. Houses were cleaned. Robes and blankets were aired. Clothes saved for special occasions were brought out. Mother made me a new dress and moccasins.

I was more interested in the food I would cook. We would have doves on a bed of wild rice. Father and Istu brought a basket filled with plump birds. We would have bitter-root noodles, squash, and corn. Mother gathered two full baskets. We would have gravy made from pine nut flour. Grandmother ground a bowl of flour. We would have berries and honey to go with cattail cakes. My sisters found juicy berries. We were ready for the Chief!

The Chief, his beautiful wife, and their handsome son arrived. The son was wearing a dashing roach—a headdress made from porcupine hair. He was twice as old as Istu.

The food was greatly enjoyed, especially the cattail cakes. Then the Chief stood up. "My oldest son, Enapay, will one day take my place as Chief of the Shoshone," he said. "He has made his decision for a wife. His mother and I pledge our support for this marriage."

The chief looked at my father and added, "If agreeable, my son would like to have your daughter become his wife in six seasons."

The air was sucked from my lungs. My legs refused to hold me up. I swayed and fell toward the fire.

Two strong arms swept me out of harm's way. "I cannot have you burn yourself, Wenona. You could not make cattail cakes for me," Enapay's soft breath brushed my cheeks. He stood me beside my father and waited.

Father looked at me and smiled. Mother gathered me in her arms. Then Father said, "You honor us, Enapay. We believe that our first daughter will make you an excellent wife. We find you an honorable and brave man. We believe you will be a good provider. It is with our blessing that we promise you Wenona in six seasons."

It was done. My life was now planned. I would marry a future Shoshone chief, one who loved my cooking as much as I loved cooking it!

The next morning I faced the sun in the east and sang a prayer song of thanks. My words were caught by rays of the sun and carried up to Appah.

Four

Shoshone Facts

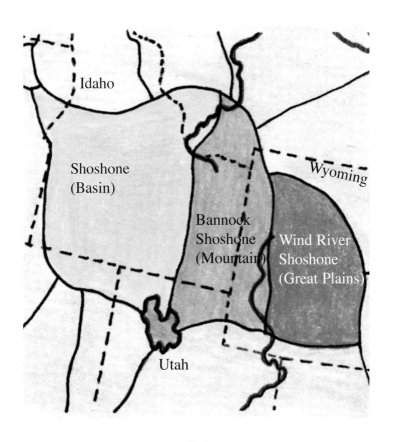

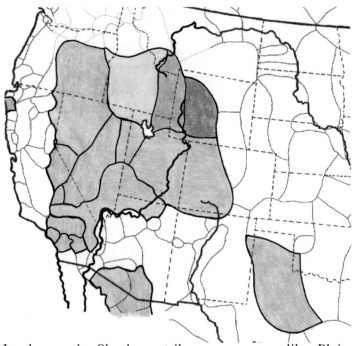

In the north, Shoshone tribes were more like Plains Indians in housing and clothing styles. Farther south, the housing became very crude because most of the country was warm all year round. There were dwellings in the mountains, the Great Basin, the southern desert, and in the far southeast. The Comanche crossed the Rockies in the north and came south into Texas.

The orange color shows the tribes that were united years ago by a common language. Now the language varies. They now use different dialects.

A crude hut made of sticks. It could have been used as a sweat lodge.

Southern tribes used curved pieces of dead wood. They placed them in a semicircle. Hides were thrown over them for shade. The houses were crude but very effective.

Most of the north-eastern Shoshone lived in tepees and wickiups. In good weather, they did not need as much shelter.

The Shoshone were very good basket makers. Some baskets were so finely made and so tight that they would hold water, and were used to cook in.

These water jugs are woven. They are covered with clay to make them more water tight.

This woven bowl and basket is a very tight weave.

This serving tray is made of woven plant fibers.

Beaded cradleboard

Leather vest with
beaded designs

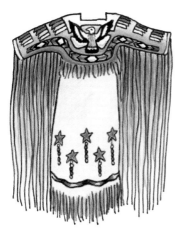

A fancy beaded dress

Shoshone woman with child

Beyond "The End"

● What have you learned to cook? When you look at a recipe, you see measurement words and procedure words. Write the words below on a sheet of paper. Circle the measurement words and draw a line under the procedure words:

cup	chop
crumble	tablespoon
ounce	pound
sift	teaspoon
cream	beat
whip	sprinkle

CURRICULUM LINKS

● Who was Sacagawea? On what coin is her picture? When was this coin put into circulation? Who is the baby shown on her back? Go to <www.usmint.gov>. Click Search. Type SACAGAWEA in the box. Click in the "Main Site" box, then click GO. Click on "Golden Dollar".

● Learn to count in Shoshone:

1	seme'
2	wahatehwe
3	bahaitee'
4	watsewite
5	manegite
6	naafaite
7	daatsewite
8	nawiwatsewite
9	seemonowemihyande
10	seemote

● The shelter described in this story was one used by the Shoshone in the summer. What were other types of shelters used by the Shoshone?

● Roaming the plains, buffalo hunters of many tribes could trade and tell hunting tales without uttering a word. They used sign language. When a Shoshone bent his elbows and held both hands with fingers drooping in front of him, it meant rainfall. Fingers near the eyes signaled weeping. Learn other sign words used by different tribes.

● Look at the Calendar of Events for Fremont County School District on the Wind River Reservation at <www.fre1.k12.wy.us>. Discuss how the schedule is different than yours; discuss how the schedule is the same as yours!

THE ARTS

● There is an art to storytelling. Read the following Shoshone legend. Learn to tell this story to younger children at your school.

One night a grizzly bear decided to go hunting in the sky. He climbed up a tall mountain. There was snow on the mountain. The snow and ice clung to Bear's feet and legs. The ice crystals trailed behind him as he crossed the sky, forming the Milky Way. Look, you can see his trail tonight!

Read some other legends of the Shoshone. Practice telling them also. Reading a story and telling a story are two very different things!

GATHERING INFORMATION

● Gathering information about cooking is different for you than it was for Wenona. You can find information about how to cook and recipes for making dishes in books, magazines, newspapers, on the Internet, and from friends.

Wenona could only learn orally from others. She did not even have a way to write down the ingredients or instructions. If you are eight years old like Wenona, how many recipes do you have stored in your memory? Okay—how many recipes for coconut cake can you gather using your methods?

THE BEST I CAN BE

● Shoshone children were taught to be very thoughtful of their guests. They always offered them something to eat. Keep in mind that food was sometimes hard to find for the Shoshone. This meant that a child might be expected to do without some of his or her food in order to have something to share with guests. They were also taught to give their guest a gift, with nothing expected in return.

You probably have much more growing up than Wenona had. Would it be hard for you to give away part of your food if you were hungry? Could you give your guest something that you treasured? Is this a good trait to teach a child today? Why?